Backyard Discovery

Benjamin sat quietly for a few moments. He looked up at the sky, but he could see only a handful of stars—even on a clear night, the bright lights of the city blocked them out. Then he heard some rustling and saw a couple of bushy tails. More squirrels, he thought. Or skunks.

But as he kept watching, he realized it was a pair of raccoons!

Books in the Jeff Corwin Series

Jeff Corwin
A Wild Life:
The Authorized Biography

Jeff Corwin
Animals and Habitats of the United States

Jeff Corwin
Junior Explorer Book 1:
Your Backyard Is Wild!

Coming Soon!
Jeff Corwin
Junior Explorer Book 2:
The Great Alaska Adventure!

JEFF CORWIN

JUNIOR EXPLORER SERIES: BOOK 1

YOUR BACKYARD IS WILD!

Illustrations by Guy Francis

PUFFIN BOOKS

An Imprint of Penguin Group (USA) Inc.

To Natasha, Maya, and Marina

PUFFIN BOOKS
Published by the Penguin Group
Penguin Young Readers Group, 345 Hudson Street, New York, New York 10014, U.S.A.
Penguin Group (Canada), 90 Eglinton Avenue East, Suite 700, Toronto, Ontario, Canada M4P 2Y3
(a division of Pearson Penguin Canada Inc.)
Penguin Books Ltd, 80 Strand, London WC2R 0RL, England
Penguin Ireland, 25 St Stephen's Green, Dublin 2, Ireland (a division of Penguin Books Ltd)
Penguin Group (Australia), 250 Camberwell Road, Camberwell, Victoria 3124, Australia
(a division of Pearson Australia Group Pty Ltd)
Penguin Books India Pvt Ltd, 11 Community Centre, Panchsheel Park, New Delhi - 110 017, India
Penguin Group (NZ), 67 Apollo Drive, Rosedale, North Shore 0632, New Zealand
(a division of Pearson New Zealand Ltd.)
Penguin Books (South Africa) (Pty) Ltd, 24 Sturdee Avenue,
Rosebank, Johannesburg 2196, South Africa

Registered Offices: Penguin Books Ltd, 80 Strand, London WC2R 0RL, England

Published by Puffin Books, a division of Penguin Young Readers Group, 2009

1 3 5 7 9 10 8 6 4 2

Text copyright © Jeff Corwin, 2009
Illustrations copyright © Guy Francis, 2009
All rights reserved

LIBRARY OF CONGRESS CATALOGING-IN-PUBLICATION DATA IS AVAILABLE.

Puffin Books ISBN 978-0-14-241404-0

Printed in the United States of America

Dear Reader,

Growing up outside of Boston, I wasn't really able to explore the natural world unless I went out into the countryside. So I had to find unique ways to discover the animals and plants around me—which led me right into my backyard! Even though I was living in a city, I found lots of amazing wildlife right outside my door. I just had to take a closer look!

And that's what the Baxter kids like to do in my Junior Explorer series—explore their immediate surroundings. Whether in a city backyard or in their hometown near the Florida Everglades, Lucy and Benjamin Baxter always find ways to discover fascinating animals and plants. And so can you! It doesn't matter where you live—all you have to do is look outside, engage your curiosity about the natural world, and have fun discovering the plants, animals, and natural life around you.

Happy exploring!

Jeff Corwin

Chapter One

The sun was rising and Daisy, a chocolate Lab, was pulling at the end of her leash.

"Please, Mom? Can't we bring her?" nine-year-old Benjamin Baxter begged as Daisy stopped to sniff a patch of grass. "Dogs go on planes all the time."

Elizabeth Baxter, Benjamin's mom, shook her head. "The city's not a good place for Daisy," she said. "She's used to being here in Florida, where she has lots of space to run. In New York, she'd have to spend most of her time indoors. And besides, it's only for a week."

Benjamin had heard this before. "But there'd be so much for her to see in New York! I know she'd love it as much as we will! And she won't get to meet Gabe." How could it be a family reunion if one member of the family was missing?

Mrs. Baxter put an arm around her son. "We'll all miss Daisy," she said. "But we'll be back before you know it, and Julie will take good care of her. She always does."

Julie was their neighbor. She had three dogs of her own. Daisy would have plenty of space to run, thought

Benjamin, but nobody to give her extra-special attention. He stroked Daisy's head gently. Leaving Daisy behind was the only bad part about their trip.

In just two hours, the Baxters would be heading off on their first-ever real family vacation. They'd taken plenty of trips before. But Benjamin's mom was a biologist, his dad was an ecologist, and most of the family's travel had to do with their jobs. They were always exploring new animal habitats or collecting samples for their labs.

This trip, though, was going to be different. They were going to New York City! They would be staying with Benjamin's cousin, Gabe, who was nine, just like Benjamin. And they would be visiting the famous sights that Benjamin had seen only in movies or in other people's photo albums.

Benjamin was excited to think that this time he'd be the kid who brought back souvenirs for his classroom. This time he'd be the one with the inside scoop on a famous museum. For him, this would be a whole new kind of adventure.

Suddenly Benjamin's mother started running down the street! Every morning they took the dog for a walk together—and every morning his mom found a different creature to watch. "Look, Benjamin!" she cried. "It's a great blue heron!" Benjamin and Daisy followed, but she had disappeared into a swamp to get a better look at the long-legged, long-necked bird.

The Baxters lived at the edge of the

Florida Everglades, a wilderness full of plants and animals you couldn't see anywhere else in the country. Benjamin's parents seemed to know everything about the different species of the Everglades, and most of the time Benjamin loved to tag along when they went exploring.

Today, though, he was totally distracted. There was a whole other world in New York just waiting for him, and he was counting the minutes until he got there.

When they got home, Benjamin's eight-year-old sister, Lucy, was just getting out of bed. "Time to get dressed," Benjamin's dad, Sam Baxter, told her when she shuffled into the kitchen. "We're almost ready to go."

Lucy was never cheerful in the morning. But she had to be excited about the trip, Benjamin figured, because today she didn't argue with their dad. She disappeared into her room and came back in a clean T-shirt and a pair of shorts, and with her hair pulled back in a neat ponytail. Lucy put her suitcase by the door and returned to the kitchen to pour herself a bowl of cereal.

"Better get your bag, too," Benjamin's dad told him. "Then we can load up the car."

Benjamin went upstairs to collect his things from his room. He'd packed a lot more than Lucy. There was the stuff he knew he had to bring: clothes and shoes, toothpaste and underwear. And then there was the stuff he really wanted to bring, such as his

camera and binoculars, his collecting
jars, his notebook and pencils, and his
magnifying glass.

He lugged his suitcase, a backpack, and a duffel bag back down the
stairs. He wasn't even at the bottom
when Lucy spoke up. "Mom said one
piece of checked baggage per person.
Remember?"

"But I need all my gear," Benjamin said. "How am I supposed to observe and record New York without it?" His parents were big believers in observing and recording. They said these were the two most important things a scientist could do: watch closely and write down what you saw.

Lucy rolled her eyes. "That's not what we're doing this time. The buildings are too tall. . . . The streets are too crowded. . . ." She crunched a bite of cereal. "And what are you going to study, anyway? People in a rush? New neighborhoods? You're not going to need all that gear for *this* trip."

Benjamin paused. He hadn't really thought of it that way. But it was like second nature to him to look at the world like a scientist. So what if he wanted to do it in New York, too? There might not be many new animals to study, but what if he wanted to observe and record other things he saw in the city? Maybe he could even write a report about them when he got home, like his parents always did after one of their nature trips.

"Just because it's not nature doesn't mean we can't take a scientific approach," Benjamin retorted.

Then his dad stepped in. "The camera and binoculars are a good idea," Mr. Baxter said, getting back to the matter of the luggage. "I'm not so sure about the other stuff . . . but maybe I can find some extra room in my bag."

Benjamin did a quick calculation. If his dad took the camera and collecting jars, he could do without the duffel bag. He would still get to bring one suitcase—the piece of checked luggage—plus his backpack as a carry-on. So he could still bring his other stuff, tucked safely under a sweatshirt in his suitcase. He needed it just in case.

By noon, the Baxters were sitting on a hot, cramped plane. They had been there for almost two hours already, and the plane still hadn't left the airport. Daisy would have hated this, thought Benjamin. He wasn't having much fun himself.

He had already eaten all the snacks he'd packed. He didn't want to run down the batteries on his MP3 player. And he was saving his books—two mysteries—for when they were really in the air. There was only one thing to do, then. Benjamin bent down, unzipped the backpack he'd stowed under the seat in front of him, and took out his binoculars. He always looked for animals when he was bored.

Lucy looked over and shook her head. "We're in the airport!" she reminded him.

"You never know what's out there," said Benjamin. He scanned the runway from the tiny plane window.

Benjamin could see baggage carriers and airport workers. He could see a line of planes ahead of theirs, waiting to take off. But it didn't take him very long to find something else.

He handed Lucy the binoculars and pointed. "Look at that radio tower," he said. "See the pile of sticks on top? I think that's an osprey's nest."

The heap of sticks looked round and even. And just as the kids were watching, a huge bird swooped into it! Even from this distance, Benjamin could tell it was an osprey by the dark mask over its face. It looked almost like a raccoon, if you ignored its five-foot wingspan. "Cool!" he said. It was the last thing he'd expected to see here.

"Let me see," their mom said excitedly, leaning across the aisle. "You know, ospreys will build their nests anywhere, so long as they're near a source of fish." She took the binoculars and looked in the direction he was pointing. "Yes, Benjamin, you're right!"

Would Gabe know an osprey nest if he saw one? Benjamin wondered. And would he be excited about it? The last time he'd seen Gabe, they'd both been five years old, in kindergarten. He hardly remembered him, except that he had dark, curly hair and a big smile.

His mom and Gabe's mom were sisters, but they lived very different lives. Benjamin worried that he and Gabe might be really different, too. What if they didn't have a good time together?

Impossible, he thought as he remembered the extra stuff he'd packed in his suitcase. First there was his rock collection—or the best rocks from his collection, really, since bringing all of them would have been too heavy. He had pieces of quartz and crystal from family exploring trips, plus smooth rocks and sharp rocks he'd found around their neighborhood. A city kid should like rocks, Benjamin thought, since you can find rocks anywhere. His collection would give him and Gabe something to talk about.

And if Gabe wasn't into rocks, Benjamin was sure he'd want to see his alligator skull! It was cast from the skull of a real alligator that his mom had in her lab. It had two rows of razor-sharp teeth and a jaw that was hinged

so it could open and close. People said that alligators lived in New York's sewers, but Benjamin was pretty sure his cousin had never seen one up close, like Benjamin had in the Everglades. It was a surefire conversation starter.

Benjamin felt better knowing that some of his treasures were coming along for the trip. Maybe, while he was learning about New York, Benjamin could also teach Gabe a thing or two about where he comes from.

Chapter Two

A few hours later, as the Baxters' plane circled above New York City preparing to land, Benjamin caught a glimpse of the famous skyline shining in the afternoon sun. It was just as he'd imagined it, only better, and he couldn't wait to see it up close! In the airport, it felt like his family waited forever for the suitcases to appear on the carousel and their turn in the taxi line to come up.

Finally, they were on their way to Gabe's house. Their cab sped along the edge of the city, and Benjamin craned his neck so he could see the tops of the buildings as they zipped by.

Suddenly Lucy was practically in his lap, trying to see for herself. "Hey, that's my arm!" Benjamin complained. "You're crushing me!"

He could see why she didn't want to miss anything, though. The skyscrapers were tall—he'd expected that. But there were so many of them! And where there weren't buildings, there were cars in traffic. Or crowds of people waiting to cross the street. The city reminded Benjamin of an ant colony. It was busy and social, like that. But much bigger, of course.

He leaned down for his backpack

again, this time to take out his notebook. "Field notes," he explained to Lucy when he saw her looking over. Their family always took notes when they were seeing something new. Real scientists tried to describe a thing carefully so they'd remember what it looked like even when they left it behind. Benjamin was sure he would *never* forget seeing New York for the first time, but he took the notes out of habit.

The taxi turned, then inched down an off-ramp. Suddenly they were on the Brooklyn Bridge! Gabe and his parents lived in Brooklyn, one of the city's five boroughs, so the Baxters had to be getting closer.

Benjamin rolled down his window and stuck his head out to see the bridge's famous archways. There were ferryboats and sailboats way down below, on the East River. Benjamin glanced at a map posted in the cab. It showed that this river fed into New York Harbor at the tip of Manhattan, just a short distance from where the bridge stood. From there, it wasn't very far to the open ocean.

The cab came off the bridge and turned onto a side street. It was quieter here, with trees lining the sidewalks. And soon they pulled in front of a building with wide steps leading up to the front door.

Benjamin saw a blur shoot out the doorway, down the stairs, and onto the sidewalk. It was Gabe! He looked a lot older but otherwise just the same as Benjamin remembered him.

Soon Gabe's parents, Aunt Lily and

Uncle Peter, were out on the sidewalk, too. Benjamin's mom and Aunt Lily gave each other a huge, sisterly hug, and the grown-ups told all the kids how big they'd grown. It was the first time they'd all been together in years. Benjamin was a little nervous and didn't know what to say to anyone.

When the conversation turned to the details of the trip, Gabe looked at Lucy and Benjamin and grimaced. "Want to see my room?" he asked. It was as if he'd just seen his cousins yesterday.

Benjamin grinned. "Let's skip this boring stuff," he said. Suddenly he wasn't nervous at all.

He and Lucy followed Gabe into the building. It was a long walk up to the fifth floor, where Gabe lived. "I thought New Yorkers had elevators,"

Benjamin said, a little out of breath.

"Some do," said Gabe. "But this building is called a walk-up. It means, you know, that you walk up!"

Gabe's place wasn't at all like the fancy New York apartments Benjamin had seen in books and TV shows. It looked comfortable, like their house at home, with a sunny living room and a cozy kitchen. There were family pictures on the walls, and Gabe's artwork on the fridge.

"My room is right in here," Gabe said, opening a door. It was small and crowded with stuff. "Want to see my collection?"

Benjamin could hardly believe his ears. He and Gabe were both nine—and they both collected stuff! "Sure. I brought a collection, too!" he said.

When his sister looked at him and rolled her eyes, Benjamin shrugged.

Gabe opened a drawer and took out six stacks of baseball cards, each secured with a rubber band. "I collect Yankees cards," he said. "Look at this one . . . it's Derek Jeter as a rookie."

The kids pored over the cards until Gabe realized one of them was missing. "Hold on," he said. "I just had it. . . . Maybe it's over here. . . ." While Gabe rummaged around his room, Benjamin took a look out the window. It faced the back of the apartment building. He could see a lot of sky and even a sliver of water. Directly below him was a patch of green.

"Hey, Gabe—what's that?" he asked.

"The backyard," said Gabe.

"A backyard!" cried Lucy. "In New York?

"Can we see?" asked Benjamin. He thought no one had those here. He couldn't wait to tell the kids back home!

"Sure," Gabe said agreeably. "Hang on a sec." He put the cards away carefully and led them back to the stairs. They went all the way down to the basement, which was dark and dusty and filled with old bikes. They passed a laundry room, and in the back there was a door that was supposed to lead outside. When Gabe pushed it, though, it was locked.

"Is there a key?" Benjamin asked. He really wanted to see the yard.

"Well . . . yeah. Somewhere. But I don't know who has it. Nobody really goes out there," he explained. "My mom says it's because nobody wants to cut the grass."

Benjamin met his sister's eye for a minute. He knew they were thinking the same thing. This was definitely one way that life in New York was different from life back home. In Florida, people spent as much time outside as they could. And they definitely didn't mind mowing a little grass!

Soon they were back in Gabe's room. "So . . . let's talk about what we're going to do this week!" Benjamin said, making red Xs on a subway map next to all the sights they wanted to see. The Statue of Liberty. The Empire State Building. The mummies at the

Metropolitan Museum. A baseball game, if they could get tickets. They couldn't do everything, but Benjamin was determined to squeeze in as much as he could.

Later that day, the Baxter kids and Gabe trailed behind their parents on a long walk through Brooklyn. Uncle Peter told the adults all about the history of the neighborhood. It was called Brooklyn Heights, and at one time it had been a suburb of New York. Now it was officially a part of the city, but it still had a quiet, old-fashioned character that set it apart.

"People like to live here," Uncle Peter said, "because it's only a short subway ride from here to downtown Manhattan. People also like the shady streets, and the smaller buildings, called brownstones because of the brown stone they're made from."

As his father continued talking to Benjamin's parents, Gabe gave his cousins his own tour. "Here's my school," he said, pointing at a brick building with a big basketball court. "Here's where my best friend lives," he noted when they passed an apartment tower. "And *this* is the best place to get ice cream."

Uncle Peter agreed. He ordered cones for the whole family, and they carried them to a path along the East River called the Promenade, where people could walk and see the skyline of lower Manhattan. After they walked for a while, Benjamin realized that the Promenade was a sort of park. But it wasn't like the parks he knew back home. That was what made it interesting.

Lucy and Benjamin posed for pictures until Benjamin said, "My ice cream is melting! Can we take a break now?" The kids sat on a bench a short distance away from their parents, right beside a playground.

Suddenly Lucy hopped down and walked toward a patch of weeds and waist-high grass. She crouched down in front of a tall plant with giant seed-pods and examined one of its leaves.

"Check this out!" she called to Benjamin and Gabe. "It's a butterfly cocoon!" The tiny brown cocoon was clinging to the underside of the leaf. You

could see it only when the breeze blew.

Gabe drew closer and looked at the cocoon. "It looks like a dead leaf to me."

"That's what cocoons always look like," Benjamin told him.

In a flash, Benjamin was beside his sister, taking his magnifying glass from the back pocket of his jeans. He had known it would come in handy! He squinted through it at the leaf. "That's a milkweed," he said. "Monarch butterflies love it. The caterpillars fill up on the leaves before they go into their cocoons." He picked a seedpod off the stem and touched the sticky white liquid that had gathered near the top of it. "Yup, definitely."

"What's it doing here?" asked Gabe.

Benjamin smiled. Gabe might know his way around Brooklyn, but he didn't know his way around the outdoors. "Milkweed grows almost everywhere," he said.

"But how do you know all this?"

Benjamin just knew. He'd known since he was a toddler. It was hard to explain, but somehow he managed to find the words.

"I know nature the way you know Brooklyn!" he said.

Chapter Three

Benjamin awoke with a start the next morning. Something wasn't right. When he opened his eyes, he knew he was at Gabe's house—that wasn't what was bothering him. Then he realized . . . it was noisy! He could hear garbage trucks rumbling in the street and people talking on their cell phones on the sidewalk five floors below. Uncle Peter had called this a quiet neighborhood, but it was louder than anywhere Benjamin had ever woken up before.

The family had bagels for breakfast—a New York specialty—and then walked to the subway station to wait for a train that would take them right into the center of New York City. They would walk from the subway stop to the Empire State Building! From the top, they would see the whole city spread out before them.

The cousins stood on the platform with their parents, and Benjamin could hear his dad telling Aunt Lily about some of the work he did as an ecologist. "And Elizabeth teaches biology in the zoology department of the local college," he heard his father say. "She studies animals and shares her research with her students. What I do is a little different, though. I study the way those animals interact with their environment."

Benjamin had heard this explanation before, so he tuned out and looked at his watch. It was hot on the platform, and there was a damp smell, too.

He felt a slight breeze. Then he heard a distant rumbling. He wondered what it was and looked at Gabe, who said, "A train."

Air-conditioned? Benjamin wondered, sweating. But the train flew through the station so fast that he couldn't even count the cars.

"An express," Gabe added. "It doesn't stop at every station."

Benjamin nodded and stared at the subway track. It was four or five feet below him, in a deep tunnel. And . . . there was something moving down there!

He nudged his sister. "Hey, Lucy," he said, pointing. "I think it's a rat!" They watched as the rat rummaged through a fast-food bag that someone had thrown on the tracks. It licked what was left inside of it, then came out with cheese on its whiskers. Soon two more rats joined it, and they scurried down the track, looking for more food.

"Oh, man," said Gabe, following his cousins' glance. "We learned about those guys in school. The rats in the subway are called Norway rats. Gross!"

Benjamin said, "I think they're kind of cool, actually. See how the color of their fur matches the color of the wood and metal of the tracks? They're camouflaged, so you don't notice them at first. But when you do, you can see there are lots of them!"

"Who'd think any animals live down here at all?" Lucy added. "They must have adapted in other ways, too."

Another train was coming—Benjamin knew the signs now. The rats disappeared into the darkness, and the subway train whooshed into the station. As the doors opened, Gabe said, "If you think they were cool, just wait till you get to the top of the world!"

Benjamin drew in his breath as he walked into the grand lobby of the Empire State Building. Its ceiling had to be two or three stories above him, and everywhere he looked there was marble.

That's when they started waiting in line. First, the security line. Then the ticket line. And then the line for the elevator to the top. After a while, even the grown-ups got restless.

Once they got up to the top, though, Benjamin realized it was all worthwhile. It was a bright, sunny day, and it seemed he could see almost all the way back to Florida. He followed Gabe through the gift shop and outside onto the observation deck.

Gabe went into tour guide mode right away. "To the west, the mighty Hudson River and the lovely skyline of New Jersey," he said, leading his cousins to one side of the building. He didn't spend much time there but motioned for his cousins to follow.

He showed them his neighborhood

to the east—they could see the Brooklyn Bridge again, this time in miniature—and the Statue of Liberty to the south. From here, the towering buildings looked like gift boxes and the cars looked like ants.

Looking north, they could see a patch of grass and trees set in the middle of the city. A pond near its edge glittered in the sunlight, and immediately Benjamin felt an urge to explore it. Gabe followed his glance and said, "Central Park, of course. Centrally located, as you can see." Benjamin made a mental note to move it to the top of his must-see list.

Gabe reached into his pocket for some quarters and fed them into a set of binoculars on a stand. Lucy looked

into them first, exclaiming, "I can see people walking on the street now—a hundred stories below. Wow!"

"This is the best way to spend your first day in the city," Gabe announced importantly. "From up here, you can see how everything fits together. And then you can visit the sights one by one." He sounded so grown-up that Benjamin wondered if his parents had said this to other visitors.

Lucy stepped down from the stand, ready to give Benjamin a turn. But Benjamin had taken out his own binoculars. He was looking at the sky!

She nudged him and teased, "Um . . . you're looking the wrong way?"

"I just thought of it," said Benjamin, "but this is an awesome place for bird-watching!" He handed his binoculars to Lucy. "Look there," he said, pointing. "Do you see the pigeons?" She didn't really need the binoculars—the pigeons were perched on a corner of the building a few stories beneath them.

Benjamin told Gabe what he knew about the birds. "You probably think they're pests," he said, "since there are so many of them in the city. But did you know they were brought to this country by European settlers, who ate them? They were considered a treat!"

"Wow," Gabe said. "That's interesting. But, you know, the big thing up here is the view."

Obviously Gabe had never been on vacation with the Baxters. They liked to learn about the local animals wherever they went. "I just think it's amazing to see the birds from up here, not from down below," Benjamin said, taking the binoculars back. As he turned around, he saw a tour group walking toward them. They were looking and pointing, and he heard someone mention the words "peregrine falcon."

"Did you hear those people talking?" Benjamin asked Gabe and Lucy.

"Somebody over there just spotted a falcon!" he exclaimed.

Benjamin found his mom and told her about the falcon—then she went off in search of someone who could tell them more. It turned out that everyone who worked at the Empire State Building knew about the wildlife in the New York skies.

"Oh, yes," a woman in a uniform confirmed. "Peregrine falcons use the building as a hunting ground. They perch on the observation deck and wait for smaller birds to fly by. Yellow-billed cuckoos, orioles, warblers, and many other birds are disoriented by the towers' lights at night. The falcons can catch them off guard!"

"What about pigeons?" Benjamin asked. "Do falcons hunt them, too?" The ones he'd seen would be easy for a falcon to catch.

"Oh, yes," the woman confirmed. "In cities, falcons help keep the pigeon population under control. Pigeons know the territory well, but falcons have superior speed. When they hunt, they fly very high, then dive down sharply toward their prey. When the falcon hits its target, it comes back and grabs it in midair. Pigeons better watch out!"

She also said that the building's lights were dimmed during certain weeks of the spring and fall, because the Empire State Building was directly in the path of flocks of migrating birds. "If the lights are at full brightness, the birds crash into the building," she said. "White-throated sparrows and common yellowthroats are some of the birds most at risk."

Benjamin quickly sketched a falcon in his notebook. Then he scribbled all the information down and tried to remember the details for when he went back to school. These were things that not many people knew about the

re . . . ," Gabe said, his sen-
ling off.

_in could tell his cousin
_ little creepy, but he couldn't
_sing in one more fact. "There
_reds of kinds of centipedes,"
"all over the world. On some
_slands, they can grow to be
_wo feet long!"

_," said Gabe. "Enough about
_atch this!"

_was still going back and forth
_monkey bars, so Gabe shinnied
_le and hung upside down on a
_ar. He did a flip and leaped to
_und. But when he landed, he
_balance! Gabe fell back and hit
_d against another bar, and his
_rumpled on the ground.

Empire State Building, not even a native New Yorker like Gabe.

Back on the street, Gabe insisted that they all buy hot dogs from a sidewalk vendor for lunch. "Another New York experience," he said. Then the families took the subway back to Brooklyn. They didn't see any rats this time, but Benjamin did hear some amazing music from the musicians in the station. Their catchy beat echoed off the tiles and made the station seem almost like a dance club!

The day was growing hotter, and the grown-ups didn't feel like doing any more sightseeing. When Gabe then suggested the playground back at the Promenade, the adults were relieved.

They sat at a picnic table in a shady spot, while the kids took turns on the monkey bars.

Waiting for his turn, Benjamin walked over to a sandbox. It looked like it hadn't been used in a while. Sticks and leaves were scattered over the sand, and some big rocks were stuck in the middle of it. Benjamin picked up one to move it. Beneath the rock, a centipede squiggled in the sand, and Benjamin picked it up.

"Gabe, come here!" he called, ready to give a tour of his own. "Look!"

Benjamin dropped the centipede into Gabe's open hand and he didn't look that thrilled about holding it. "What's that?" Gabe asked, a bit suspiciously. "A baby snake?"

"Nope," Benjamin replied. "A

centipede! worm. But a salamand is divided each with its

Gabe studi antennae, to claws?" Nice thought.

"They are," in woodsy, m not vegetarian to catch and ki insects. In his predator!" Whi ber something better put that They can pinch

His cousin dr like a hot potato.

here befo tence trai

Benjam found it resist tos are hund he said, Pacific almost t

"Okay bugs! W

Lucy on the up a p high b the gr lost his his he body

Chapter Four

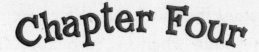

Benjamin crouched down next to his cousin. "Are you okay?" he asked anxiously. He didn't know what to do!

Luckily, Lucy and the grown-ups were beside him in seconds, and Aunt Lily smoothed Gabe's hair back off his forehead until he could speak. He was a little dizzy, which worried his mom. But after a while, he stood up and seemed to be fine.

Aunt Lily and Uncle Peter weren't taking any chances, though. They hailed a taxi, while Benjamin's family walked back to the apartment. Benjamin couldn't help but wonder what this would mean for their trip. Would Gabe still be able to do all the things they'd planned?

Back at the apartment, Gabe was already on the couch, resting. A woman was sitting beside him, and Uncle Peter told Benjamin it was one of their neighbors, a doctor at a nearby hospital.

"You must have taken quite a fall!" she said to Gabe, keeping the tone light. "You might want to think twice before you try that trick again!"

She got more serious as she explained that head injuries had to be treated with care. "It doesn't seem like you have a concussion, which is good," she said. "All I can see is a bump at the back of your head, which we can keep down with ice. But you're going to need to take it easy for a couple of days."

Gabe groaned. "But I have things to do!" he said. "I can't just lie on the couch while my cousins are here!"

"We'll stay with you," Benjamin promised. It wasn't what he'd expected from the trip, but spending time with Gabe was more important than anything else.

And this would be a perfect time to show Gabe his rock collection! He was able to distract Gabe for a while by showing him many different kinds of rocks and telling him where they'd come from.

Gabe also laughed when Lucy

brought out the alligator skull, moved its jaws, and made it say, "Get well soon, Gabe!"

"That thing is amazing!" Gabe said, looking it over. "I need to get one of those!"

Eventually, though, Gabe got back to talking about their visit. "It's not fair," he complained. "What are we supposed to do now? Watch movies about New York instead of explore the real thing?"

That's when Benjamin was inspired. "What if we do a different kind of sight-seeing? The kind we Baxters always do on trips?" When Gabe stared at him blankly, he explained a little more. "Usually we watch animals and explore where they live. Usually we're part of our parents' research trips, so we end up doing research ourselves."

"Okay . . . but how are we supposed to do that here?" Gabe asked doubtfully. "I think we've seen all the animals there are to see."

"No way," Lucy said. "I'll bet there's a whole lot more for us to find."

"Wildlife isn't exactly what makes New York famous," Gabe pointed out. "But I guess it would be okay to try. Where do we start?"

Benjamin smiled. "Well . . . can you get that key to the backyard?"

It took until the next afternoon for them to find out that the key was hanging in another neighbor's kitchen. And Aunt Lily thought it would be great for Gabe to get some fresh air, as long as he wasn't roughhousing outside. As soon as they got the key, Benjamin grabbed his backpack and the three cousins tromped down to the basement again. The grown-ups could watch them from the upstairs window.

Lucy turned the key in the lock and pushed open the door to the yard. It squeaked on its hinges, like it hadn't been used in a while. The cousins climbed up three steps and blinked in the afternoon light.

"Oh, man," said Gabe. "Look at the grass!" It was at least knee-high and looked like it hadn't been mowed in a couple of months. There was a brick path to the fence at the back of the property and a raised flower bed that

needed weeding. There were old flow-
erpots scattered around the yard, too.

"It's perfect!" Lucy exclaimed. "The
wilder, the better."

"So, what now?" Gabe asked.

"Our parents have one rule," Benjamin said. "We're supposed to keep
quiet. It's so we can hear any animals
coming toward us—and not scare
them away if they are."

Gabe nodded. "I can do that," he
said.

Benjamin sat on the steps and lis-
tened. The city was so much noisier
than the swamp back home. He could
hear all the sounds that had surprised him before, plus even more.
There was the blast of a ferry whistle
out on the water, and the chopping

of a helicopter. Benjamin wondered
if that noise alone would scare away
any animals. Then, suddenly, he heard
something else. A rustling in the leaves
above him. He looked up and saw a
New York squirrel! He didn't know exactly what kind it was, but it was medi-
um size and gray, and it was watching
him with its shiny black eyes.

The squirrel hopped down off a low tree branch and perched on the side of a large flowerpot. With its front feet, it dug in the dirt until it found what it wanted: some seeds.

Slowly, Benjamin handed Gabe the binoculars so he could watch the squirrel eating the seeds one by one in the grass. When the squirrel was through, it hopped a few feet away and dug another small hole in the ground. There was an acorn buried there! The boys observed as the squirrel gnawed on it, then bounded away.

"All right . . . I've never done that before," Gabe practically whispered. He seemed in awe of what had just happened. "I've seen thousands of squirrels before, but I never really watched one."

"Did you see how it knew where the acorn was?" Benjamin asked. "Squirrels have a very accurate memory for where they've hidden their food. They bury nuts and seeds in thousands of places every year, and they can always find them!"

"I guess I've never really thought about it before . . . ," Gabe said, trailing off.

"When you're a backyard explorer, you see things a little differently!" Benjamin announced. He dug through the flowerpot for the seeds the squirrel had left behind. Then he popped them into one of his plastic collecting jars. Later, he'd ask his parents what they were.

Benjamin wandered over to the flower bed next. If he was an explorer, that seemed like exciting new territory. He could see where daffodils had bloomed in the spring—their stalks were still there—and where someone had even tried to plant a few vegetables. Some tomato stalks were climbing up a pole, but there were just nubs where there should have been hard, green tomatoes ready to ripen. Benjamin was sure another animal had stolen them.

He stood by the flower bed for several minutes, waiting and watching. Just when he was ready to move to another part of the yard, a delicate snake crossed in front of him and went to bask on a low stone wall! "Look, a garter snake," Benjamin hissed to his sister and his cousin.

He wanted to pick it up—he was pretty sure that the worst a garter snake

could do was give off a bad smell—but he didn't want to take any chances. Instead, he motioned Gabe and Lucy over to take a look. The garter snake had a striped pattern on its skin, and between the stripes were rows of dots.

"Garter snakes live all over the place," Lucy told Gabe. "They're one of the most common snakes around."

As they watched, the snake slithered to the end of the wall. In a moist, shady spot, it found a couple of slugs.

Then, with one gulp, the snake swallowed one of them!

"I can't believe it," Gabe said, shaking his head. "The food chain . . . right here in the yard."

It was funny to see Gabe so surprised, Benjamin thought. The look on Gabe's face was probably like the look *he'd* had when they were in the subway station. They watched the snake slide through a fence to the next yard.

Now Benjamin brought out a small shovel and handed it to Gabe. Benjamin was glad he'd managed to fit so many supplies in his backpack! "Let's see what we can dig up next," he joked. The boys took turns digging in a pile of old leaves. The ones on top were dry and crunchy, but the ones underneath were moist and decomposing.

Soon Benjamin found yet another creature. It was small, and had rolled into a ball when he picked it up. "Look, a pill bug," he said, handing it to Lucy.

"Also known as a roly-poly," she confirmed. "Look at this one, Gabe!"

She held it out for him to see.

Gabe gasped as the ball unrolled in her palm, revealing an oval body with seven pairs of legs. Its back was a hard shell made of several different pieces.

"You'll never guess who his cousins are!" said Benjamin.

"Armadillos?" Gabe replied.

"Crabs and lobsters," Benjamin said, chuckling. "Crustaceans. It looks like an insect, but the pill bug is actually the only crustacean that lives entirely on land. It doesn't need to be in water; but it likes dark, wet places, like the leaf pile."

"Unbelievable!" Gabe said.

For a moment, Benjamin thought he saw Gabe's attention wander, and suddenly he wondered if his cousin was overwhelmed. He knew what it felt like when his parents tried to show him everything at once. When they did that, he always wished they could take a break. And that was when he hadn't had a bad accident on a playground!

"I think we've explored enough for now," Benjamin said to Gabe and Lucy. "Let's go inside for a snack!"

Chapter Five

The minute they got inside, Gabe wanted to go back out again! Benjamin realized he was all wrong about his cousin needing a break. In fact, Gabe couldn't get enough of exploring the yard! "It's like *they're* showing *me* around," he heard him say to Aunt Lily. "It's a part of New York I never even knew was there!"

They couldn't go back out yet,

though, because Uncle Peter had made dinner. "My famous lasagna," he said, putting a piece on every plate.

As they ate, Gabe asked the Baxters about the exploring trips they'd taken. Benjamin's parents didn't even know where to start. "Well, we went to Yellowstone last summer," said Mrs. Baxter. "At home, we'd been studying the endangered species of the Everglades. Out west, though, different species are threatened. We did some research on wolves while we were there."

"For a long time there were almost no wolves left," Benjamin added. "But now scientists and conservationists are working to bring them back."

"I think that was my favorite trip ever," Lucy said. "I mean, besides this one. We got to see the wolves up close—they acted just like dogs! Plus we spent a whole week camping!"

"I've never been camping," Gabe said.

"We'll have to take you sometime," replied Benjamin. "Maybe when you come to Florida." It was another thing he could show his cousin!

But Gabe had another idea. "How about we camp out in the backyard tonight?" he asked.

His mother frowned. "I don't think so, Gabe," she said. "It's not safe. . . . And we don't even have a tent."

"But could we go out there after dark?" Benjamin asked. "Just for a little while? If a grown-up is watching us? We can see all kinds of other animals then."

Gabe's mom hesitated for a minute. Then Benjamin's dad said, "I'll go with them, Lily. I'll make sure they're all right."

Aunt Lily smiled. "It's fine by me, then."

"Hooray!" shouted Gabe. He sounded as excited as Benjamin had felt the morning they left home.

The summer was almost over, and the days were getting shorter. Still, it was after 9:00 before the sky was completely dark. The kids followed Mr. Baxter out the basement door. They still had Benjamin's backpack with them, full of collecting jars and tools for digging. And this time each kid had a flashlight, too.

The yard looked different in the

dark, Benjamin thought. It was full of mysterious shadows and patterns now. Even the sounds were different.

Benjamin walked down the brick path and knocked over a flowerpot by mistake. His dad put his finger to his lips, reminding him to be quiet. Benjamin put up his hands—his way of saying, It was an accident!

He swept his flashlight over a small patch of ground in front of him. There was some movement between the bricks—it was hard to see, but he was pretty sure there was a beetle down there. And what was that, hidden in the tall grass? Benjamin bent to pick it up, then brought it to his cousin so they could examine it together.

"What is it? It looks like a bunch of sticks," Gabe whispered. It had a

rounded shape, and it was just the right size to carry something small and delicate.

"It's a bird's nest," Benjamin replied. "It probably blew out of a tree!" It was amazing to think of the tiny eggs that had been in there once—or of the baby birds that had since flown away.

"Wait a minute!" Gabe said. "There's something else in the grass, too." He took a few steps and shone his flashlight near where Benjamin had found the nest. He picked up something and stared at it, mystified. It was a small fleck of something, like a seashell or a thin piece of soap.

This time Gabe was the one who realized what they were looking at. "That's a shell from a hatched egg!" he cried. His voice was low, but Benjamin could tell Gabe was excited and proud.

"Nice going, Gabe!" he said. Then he called his dad over, softly. "Dad, look at this eggshell we found. Any idea what kind of bird laid the egg?" he asked.

Mr. Baxter shone his flashlight on it and examined it carefully. "See that pale blue color that's almost faded away?" he said. "That's the trademark color of a robin's egg."

A little while later, a shadow slinked into the yard from around the neighbor's fence. At first Benjamin thought it was a black-and-white cat . . . until he realized it was a skunk!

"Don't worry," he told Gabe, who was looking worried enough for both of them. "Skunks don't like to use their spray—it's sort of a last resort for them. They don't want to use it all up, since they only carry enough for five or six sprays and it takes a while for their bodies to build it up again. If we don't bother him, he won't bother us."

Benjamin knew that what he said was true, but he was still glad when the skunk slipped under the same fence as the garter snake. There was no telling what other animals might do to rile the skunk, and he didn't want to be anywhere near it if it sprayed!

"Hey, where's Lucy?" he asked all of a sudden. The yard wasn't very big. So where could she be?

A soft whisper came from around the corner of the house. "Over here!"

"I'll be right back," Benjamin said to Gabe and his father. He followed the sound to a small wooden enclosure where there were several trash cans. It looked like there were enough for Gabe's whole building there.

"What are you doing?" Benjamin asked his sister. It was just like her to leave the main action and focus in on some sideshow.

"Waiting," she said.

"For what?"

"Just watch," Lucy replied. "You'll see."

Benjamin sat quietly for a few moments. He looked up at the sky, but he could see only a handful of stars—even on a clear night, the bright lights of the city blocked them out. Then he heard some rustling and saw a couple of bushy tails. More squirrels, he thought. Or skunks.

But as he kept watching, he realized it was a pair of raccoons! Their eyes

shone brightly through the dark masks on their faces. They looked like a couple of bandits from the Wild West, but Benjamin knew that scientists thought the dark fur served a real purpose, such as blocking glare and enhancing the raccoons' night vision.

The raccoons hopped into the trash enclosure and onto the rows of cans. Then, one by one, they tried to take off the tops. Most of the tops were securely fastened . . . but one of them was not.

The larger raccoon pried it off with its nose and tossed it aside. Then it began to rip into a trash bag with its paws! Soon somebody's leftovers were all over the ground, and the raccoons were having a feast.

Benjamin went back to get their

dad, who walked over in the dark with Gabe.

"I thought they ate, you know, fish," Gabe said. "So why do they bother with people's garbage?"

"Raccoons are extremely clever animals," said Mr. Baxter. "More than most mammals, they have totally adapted to life in the city. They eat fish—or crawfish, really—when they can. But they are just as happy with somebody's leftover fish dinner! They will eat frogs or insects, too—raccoons change to fit whatever environment they're in. It's not good for them to eat humans' trash, though," he added. "It's dangerous for them to become too domesticated and lose their wild instincts."

"What if that's our trash?" Gabe

said. "My mom won't be too happy if she knows I watched this happen!"

His words startled the raccoons, and they were gone as quickly as they'd come.

"Let's clean it up," said Mr. Baxter in his normal voice. "I think it's about time we went in anyway. Just put everything back in the cans—I'll come out and rebag it all later. It's the first rule of being outdoors: leave everything just as you found it."

Gabe nodded, taking it all in.

But Lucy joked, "Why don't you tell that to the raccoons?"

Chapter Six

Two days later, Aunt Lily and Uncle Peter decided they could stop worrying about Gabe. He had followed doctor's orders and stayed close to home, exploring the backyard and playing games and watching movies inside. But now they thought it was safe for him to get back to showing his cousins around town.

Benjamin was ready to get back to it,

too. He and the other kids had collected plants and rocks. They had observed countless creatures in Gabe's backyard. But there was still a big city out there that he wanted to see!

Today they were going to visit the American Museum of Natural History. The two families crammed into Aunt Lily's minivan—this time they were driving instead of taking the subway. Once they crossed the bridge again, Uncle Peter said, "How about we take a detour through Times Square?"

Benjamin had seen Times Square once on TV, when his parents let him stay up late on New Year's Eve. He remembered its dizzying bright lights, its happy crowds, and the clouds of confetti they tossed into the air at midnight. When they drove through Times

Square, Benjamin couldn't believe this was a "normal" day! The lights and the crowds were still there—all that was missing was the confetti. It was like every day was a celebration in New York.

Uncle Peter drove up the west side of Central Park, past a majestic building with tall columns and another crowd out front. "That's the museum! There are dinosaur bones and models of huge ocean creatures and a planetarium in there. You guys will love it!" Gabe told Benjamin and Lucy as Uncle Peter parked the car.

But Benjamin was already having some doubts. The line to get in was long. And it was a beautiful day—the kind of day when his family would usually be outdoors. He didn't want to be rude, but he just had to ask . . . "Could we go to Central Park instead?" he suggested. "It's so nice out, and I'd rather see nature alive than nature in a museum!"

His mom winked at him, and he wondered if she'd been thinking the same thing. She added, "I've been dying to visit the park since we saw it from the top of the Empire State Building."

That quickly, it was decided.

The families entered Central Park just as a pair of horses trotted by, pulling an old-fashioned carriage behind them. There were pathways full of runners and bikers. And between them all were patches of grass, some small and some massive, with people reading books or playing ball. It was the busiest park Benjamin had ever seen.

As usual, the kids ran ahead while

the parents strolled slowly behind. And soon they were standing in front of the last thing Benjamin ever expected to see in the middle of the city: a lake! People were paddling around on rowboats, taking pictures of the famous buildings that were reflected in the water.

"Oh, we have to rent a boat!" Gabe said. "It's the only way we'll be able to see what this lake is really like." It was as if, after a few days with his cousins, he was starting to think like them.

Each family went rowing in one boat. Across the water, Benjamin could hear his uncle telling Gabe about the history of the park. But Benjamin's parents, as usual, were focused on the wildlife.

"Benjamin—look," his mom said. She pointed to a pile of rocks near

shore. Benjamin couldn't see what made them special until they rowed a little closer. That's when he realized they weren't rocks at all but a bunch of turtles basking in the sun! "Eastern painted turtles," his mom said before he had a chance to ask. She knew by the pattern on their shells. "They're sitting in the sun because they're cold-blooded and can't regulate their own body temperature. A good sunbath will keep them warm for a while, though."

The Baxters rowed up to Gabe's boat, then pointed their oars so his family could see the turtles. "I just read online that a thirty-pound snapping turtle lives in this lake, too!" Aunt Lily said cheerfully. "He was discovered when some workers had to drain a portion of the lake."

Benjamin was curious about that one! Snapping turtles were a little more ferocious than other turtles, and thirty pounds was pretty big! He looked for it as he paddled, but there was no sign of it. He did notice a group of mallard ducks and a flock of Canada geese, though. He also saw frogs leaping through in the greenery around the shoreline, though they moved too quickly for him to tell what kind they were. He knew they were frogs, not toads, since they had long legs for hopping and smooth, greenish skin. The skin of toads tended to be browner and drier, and their legs were short and stubby.

When their arms were tired from rowing, the families walked across the park to the East Side and the Central Park Zoo. Benjamin, Lucy, and Gabe spent a long time watching the sea lions at feeding time. They leaped out of the water and snatched fish from their trainers' hands.

One sea lion even hopped on the rocks and walked on his flippers for the crowd. The trainer smiled proudly at his student, and Benjamin knew how he felt. It was the way he felt, back home, whenever he taught Daisy a new trick.

Later, the cousins sat on a bench outside the zoo, watching the cars and buses drive down Fifth Avenue. Their parents lined up at another street vendor, this time to buy them hot pretzels.

Benjamin caught sight of a woman on the other side of the street walking seven dogs. Were they all hers? he wondered.

"A dog walker," Gabe told him, following his gaze. "That's her job. She takes care of the pets while their owners are at work." Only in New York, thought Benjamin. Daisy would never stand for that!

Then Benjamin watched a bunch

of pigeons pecking at the pavement, eating every crumb they could find. Like raccoons, pigeons were perfectly adapted to life in the city, though some people considered them pests.

Just then, Gabe jumped off his bench and pointed into the air. "Pale Male!" he shouted.

Lucy looked to Benjamin for an answer, but he had no idea what Gabe was talking about. He couldn't even see what Gabe was pointing to.

And then . . . there it was. A magnificent hawk soaring above Fifth Avenue, hovering above the bus fumes and the tour groups until it landed on the roof of a building across the street.

"Was that . . . ?" Lucy asked.

"A red-tailed hawk!" Benjamin cried. He could tell by its broad wingspan and its distinctive red tail feathers.

"What's he doing here?" Lucy wondered.

"He lives here," Gabe said.

Both cousins turned to look at him. Gabe wasn't usually the expert on animals or nature. But this time, he had a lot to tell them.

"Lots of famous people live in the city," Gabe said. "But Pale Male is one of the most famous animals—so famous that I've read about him in school."

"Well, what's his story?" Benjamin prompted his cousin.

"Pale Male moved to New York about fifteen years ago," Gabe said. "Or that's what the experts think. Bird-watchers saw him building a nest in Central Park, but he didn't last long

there because he was chased away by crows. That's when he moved across the street! He perched on an apartment building instead of in a tree and built his nest in some fancy stonework above a window."

"So he still lives there?" Lucy asked.

"Now he does," replied Gabe. "But not without a fight. The owners of the apartment building tried to make changes to the stonework . . . until people complained. Pale Male and his mate had raised many chicks in that nest, and they'd become part of the neighborhood. Nobody wanted to see them hurt or moved. So now they're back in their old nest."

"And that was really him?" Lucy asked, as breathlessly as if she'd seen a movie star.

"I'm not really sure," Gabe admitted. "But red-tailed hawks are unusual in New York. If it wasn't him, it definitely could have been another bird in his family."

"That's an awesome story," Benjamin said.

Gabe grinned. "I never paid much attention to it before. You know . . . it's like the animals in my yard. I never paid attention to them—I hardly knew they were there. You guys have shown me a whole new side of the city. I was supposed to be *your* tour guide! But I'll never see New York in the same way."

Benjamin thought back to what he'd imagined his trip would be like. He'd thought it would be all about the city's famous landmarks, but instead it was all about seeing the city's natural wonders. It wasn't what he had expected—it was even better. And he would never see New York in the same way again, either!

Before he went to bed that night, Benjamin took out his notebook. Observe and record: it was like his family's mantra, an easy way to re-member how scientists always looked at the world. Benjamin realized he'd done a lot more observing than record-ing on this trip. He'd been too busy having fun! He didn't want to forget anything he'd learned, though. And he didn't want to forget even one detail that he might share with his classmates back home.

He opened the notebook and turned to the pages where he'd done some quick sketches of animals. Now it was time to write about them. To write about all of New York, actually . . . he didn't know where to begin!

Benjamin chewed his eraser and thought about the most exciting place he'd seen in the city. It wasn't the sub-way or the Empire State Building,

Brooklyn Heights or even Central Park. It was a place that few tourists would see, but a place that contained some of the city's greatest surprises.

He turned to a new page and wrote the name of it across the top: *Your Backyard Is Wild!* And then he went to work!